Christmas

Terror Tales

Stories to Enjoy From
October Through December

Written by Kevin M. Folliard

Illustrated by J.T. Molloy

Dedicated to the next generation
of horror enthusiasts…

CONTENTS

ACKNOWLEDGMENTS

Special thanks to my wonderful network of writer friends who helped me refine this compilation.

THE CHRISTMAS JACK-O-LANTERN

Mrs. Fellows was the most extravagant decorator in the neighborhood. Every October her house was decked out with pumpkins, witches, skeletons, fake spiders, and plastic webs. But Halloween was just the opening act. Once the calendar reached November 1st, she immediately took down all of her ghosts and ghouls and swapped them for lights and snowmen. She couldn't wait to shift holidays and put up the family Christmas tree with all the trimmings as early as possible. The front of the house positively glowed with lights and animatronics. There were elves, santas, reindeer, the Three Kings, shepherds, angels, and a nativity scene with every barnyard animal imaginable. Upon the chimney, Mr. Fellows mounted a gleaming Star of David and the sidewalk was lined with cardboard carolers with mounted speakers playing cheerful holiday tunes.

Because of her impeccable taste, Mrs. Fellows was made head of the neighborhood decorating committee, and every December each street competed in a holiday decoration contest. It was Mrs. Fellows's duty to spread holiday cheer by encouraging everyone on her block to participate, coordinate their decorations, and ensure her sterling reputation by winning.

One year, after Halloween had ended and Mrs. Fellows had erected her entire Christmas monument inside and out, she noticed the neighbor across the street had left his Jack-O-Lantern on the front stoop. The Jack-O-Lantern was expertly carved with sinister triangular eyes and a wide jagged grin. She had admired it last week, but now she found the sight of it distressing.

1

"That Jack-O-Lantern is overstaying its welcome," she remarked to her husband as she peered out from behind the curtain. "It's almost a week old, and it's going to rot."

"So what?" Mr. Fellows shrugged from the sofa, engrossed in the TV. "Not everybody switches from Halloween to Christmas like you. There's a whole other holiday in between. Pumpkins are fine for November."

"Regular pumpkins are." Mrs. Fellows glared. "Not Jack-O-Lanterns. I'm going to have a talk with him."

"Let it go, Martha," Mr. Fellows groaned.

"It's my job. I'll be polite as peaches." Mrs. Fellows marched across the street, her head held high. She sneered down at the Jack-O-Lantern as she knocked upon her neighbor's door.

A thin balding man with a cigarette in his mouth answered. "Yep?"

"Hello, I'm Mrs. Fellows from across the street. I'm the head of the neighborhood decorating committee, and I couldn't help but notice this charming little Jack-O-Lantern."

The man grinned and took a puff of his cigarette. "I'm proud of this little bugger. Carved him myself."

"Of course, you have quite a talent." Mrs. Fellows clicked her tongue from behind her bared teeth. "I just thought I'd remind you about the Christmas decoration contest. You've only lived on our street a few months, and it's coming right up!"

"Hmmm…" The man flicked ash down onto his front stoop.

"And well…" Mrs. Fellows cleared her throat, "it seems that this little guy is rotting, and we want to have a strong presentation from now until Christmas."

"It ain't Christmas yet." The man gave her a cockeyed glare. "And he ain't rottin'. Looks fine as can be."

"Well... he'll be rotting soon." Mrs. Fellows tossed her hands up in the air and gave a haughty laugh. "Just a friendly reminder."

"Afternoon." The man slammed the door in her face.

Mrs. Fellows glared at the smiling Jack-O-Lantern and crossed the street in a huff. All November long she coordinated with her friends on the decorating committee. Many of them followed her example putting up their Christmas decorations early, and each house that Mrs. Fellows advised became a shining example to the other neighbors. But the Jack-O-Lantern across the street remained. To add further insult, the man even had the nerve to light it at night. Its terrible grinning face glowed at her beautifully decorated home all evening long. She waited and waited for the Jack-O-Lantern to rot and collapse. But strangely it did no such thing. It remained as sharp and sturdy as it had been in mid-October.

"It must be plastic," Mrs. Fellows deduced one night as she studied its gleaming eyes and mouth. "It's a plastic Jack-O-Lantern with a bulb inside. Not sure how I didn't notice that."

"Stop obsessing over that darn Jack-O-Lantern," Mr. Fellows snapped. "The man can decorate his house however he wants."

"It's a mockery of the spirit of the season," she insisted.

"It isn't even Thanksgiving yet," Mr. Fellows said. "He'll put it away at the end of the month."

"He had better," Mrs. Fellows snapped.

The day after Thanksgiving, Mrs. Fellows waited anxiously by the window for the man to take in his Jack-O-Lantern. But when night came and again the eerie yellow glow of its mouth and eyes lit up the man's front stoop, she became incensed. She stalked across the street and rapped upon the man's door. The man's eyes glazed over when he saw her. "Tis the season to be jolly!" Mrs. Fellows sang. "Not spooky. Halloween is over. Thanksgiving is over. It's time to take our little friend inside."

"How come?" The man said with little interest as he lit up a cigarette.

"Because Christmas comes but once a year and everyone in the neighborhood competes to have the brightest most cheerful displays. You know, I have an old wooden sleigh I don't put out anymore that you could borrow, and we have plenty of lights we could loan you. My husband would put them up on your bushes!"

"No thanks," the man smiled. "I'm happy with my little guy here." He took a long drag and flicked his glowing cigarette onto his lawn. "Goodnight." He shut his door.

Mrs. Fellows growled under her breath. She stooped down to examine the hideous Jack-O-Lantern. It didn't appear to be plastic at all. She peered inside its devious jagged mouth to see if it was lit by a bulb or a candle and could only see a bright yellow glow. As she stood up to walk away, something viciously clamped onto her ankle. Mrs. Fellows screamed as the pumpkin's mouth pierced and burned her skin. She kicked and shrieked until it finally released her foot. She hobbled across the street panting and moaning and raved to her husband when she returned. "That horrible Jack-O-Lantern across the street bit me!"

Mr. Fellows examined the burns and puncture marks on her ankle. "You've got to stop obsessing about this Jack-O-Lantern. It's making you a little nuts."

"But look at what it's done!"

4

"You probably stuck your foot in there by accident. It's full of candles I'll bet. You've got to leave this whole thing alone."

As it turned out, Mrs. Fellows had twisted her ankle escaping the Jack-O-Lantern and spent the month of December hobbling about on a cane. All month long the Jack-O-Lantern remained on her neighbor's front stoop glowing and grinning at her from across the street. Her husband and the doctor refused to believe her, but she knew better. When she turned her back on it she could almost hear it. Snickering like a naughty little trick-or-treater. Refusing to accept that Halloween had come and gone. It made her furious. Not celebrating Christmas was one thing. But this man's insistence on leaving his little glowing friend out there to bite the neighbors was an act of war.

When the first snow fell, the Jack-O-Lantern's face glowed resiliently behind a white pile, slowly melting a little puddle around it. Its fire would not die. Its flesh would not rot. And its nasty little grin would never quit. Every other house on the street had put up their Christmas decorations by now, but the Jack-O-Lantern remained the one eyesore staining their perfect holiday paradise. Mrs. Fellows had never lost the decorating contest, and as head of the committee, it was her duty to ensure perfection on her street. The man and his Jack-O-Lantern had assaulted both her and the neighborhood, and she would make them pay.

"I want you to go out there in the middle of the night and smash it!" she instructed her husband. "Smash it to bits. But be careful, because it has razor sharp reflexes."

"You're getting goofy, Martha," Mr. Fellows said. "If you don't cut this Jack-O-Lantern nonsense out, I'm calling the men in white coats to take you away."

Mrs. Fellows decided that if her husband would not help her, she would take care of things herself. She crafted a polite but firm note, using letters she cut out of her decorating magazines, warning her neighbor to remove his Jack-O-Lantern before the night of December 18th, the night before the decorating committee passed judgment.

On the morning of the 18th, Mrs. Fellows found several of her cardboard characters in shambles on the front lawn. Jagged, triangular shapes had been bitten out of them, decapitating children, and mangling angels. An animatronic chicken was missing from her manger scene as well. Mrs. Fellows's eyes tracked its vinyl feathers across the street to the devious glowing grin of the Jack-O-Lantern. She had had enough!

That night at midnight, she hobbled across the street and stood within arms' reach of the terrible little monster. She planted her feet as best she could, raised her cane high into the air, then struck downwards with all her might. The Jack-O-Lantern rolled onto its back and bit her cane ferociously, dripping hot spittle upon the wood, setting it ablaze. She screamed and fell backwards in the snow as the Jack-O-Lantern chomped her cane into cinders. She shouted and cursed as she struggled forwards and grabbed the hideous creature's jaws with both hands. Her fingers burned in the Jack-O-Lantern's blazing mouth as she pried its upper and lower jaw open as far as she could until the entire pumpkin pulled apart in an explosion of orange flesh and yellow fire. Her hands bled and burned, and her ankle throbbed as she sat in the snow amidst the remains of the Jack-O-Lantern and chuckled triumphantly. She climbed back onto her feet and limped as best she could towards the street, laughing all the way. As she struggled across the street without her cane, she came upon a slick patch of ice and slipped onto her back, hitting her head hard. She lay helpless in the middle of the road, unable to get up.

    She turned towards her immaculate house and smiled with pride at the colorful city of holiday cheer. Then she slowly turned her head the other way, feeling extraordinary relief that she had purified the neighborhood just in time for Christmas. The front door of the neighbor's house slowly opened and the man stooped down, placing a brand new Jack-O-Lantern with the same jagged smile on his front stoop. He lit a cigarette, then discarded the match into the pumpkin's mouth lighting it with a bright yellow flare. He grinned, waved, and took a long drag of smoke.

"Happy Holidays!" he called out from his front door.

Mrs. Fellows moaned in frustration and tilted her head back on the icy concrete as she drifted into unconsciousness.

HOME FOR THE HOLIDAYS

A young college boy walked along a country road at night as a heavy snow fell. The silhouette of an old rusty semi-truck appeared behind two high beams of light. The boy waved the truck down, and a large trucker leaned over to open the passenger door. "Goin' my way?"

The boy climbed inside. "Thank you very much. I'm trying to make it home for the holidays and surprise my family. Every year we have an enormous feast."

The trucker shook the boy's hand with a fat greasy palm, and pulled back onto the road. "You're a long way from anything, kid. Could have frozen to death out there."

"I know," the boy replied. "My car broke down, and I have no phone. But I had to make it home for Christmas dinner." The boy was clean, well-dressed, and sporting a warm friendly smile. He took out a leather wallet and opened it, revealing many large bills. He offered the trucker one of them. "For your trouble."

"Oh, I don't need your money," the trucker said. "I'm just happy for the company. Nobody should be alone this time of year."

The boy rubbed his hands together in front of the heater. "Thanks. Where are you headed tonight?"

The trucker laughed. "It's just me and the road. I have no family."

"I'm sorry," the young man swallowed nervously. "Would you like to come back with me to my parents' house for dinner then? We would all be happy to have you."

The trucker rolled down his window and spat. "I'm not much of a people person." He locked his doors and took a right turn down a dirt road into the forest.

"Are you sure you know where you're going?" The boy asked.

"Oh yes," the trucker whispered. "I've been up and down these old roads many times. This is a shortcut."

They sat in silence as the main road disappeared further and further behind them. The dirt path led through the trees and into a crusty gray cornfield. There was no light in any direction save the beams of the truck. "I don't feel well," the boy said finally. "I think I'd like to get out here."

"But there's nothing around for miles." The trucker smiled.

"That's okay," the boy stuttered. "I need fresh air."

The trucker pulled over slowly and unlocked the doors. The boy leapt out of the truck and bent over at the side of the road. The trucker followed him and placed his pudgy hands around the boy's neck. "You're going to be all right, son," the trucker said. "Just relax."

The boy turned and stabbed the trucker in his enormous belly. The trucker gagged, then fell into the snow. The young man licked the blood off his fingers and smacked his lips. "I'm going to have to insist that you join us for dinner," he said. "It's just not a feast without the main course."

MANGER BABY

Jessica knew that if she stole the wooden baby Jesus from the church nativity scene, everyone in town would be furious. So on the way home from school, when nobody was around, she swiped it and hid it in her bag.

Later that evening, Jessica's mother informed the family that Jesus was gone. Everybody in town was just as enraged as Jessica knew they would be. Jessica's teacher asked anyone who knew anything about the crime to come forward and confess. That Sunday at church, the priest gave a long talk about why the thief should return Jesus and ask for forgiveness. But Jessica did not confess, or want forgiveness. The whole thing was very funny to her. She liked to see everyone worked up over a silly wooden baby.

Jessica's mother had called the thief ignorant. But Jessica knew that wasn't true. She was in fact very clever because nobody had caught her, and nobody would ever find the wooden baby in the crawl space behind her closet. She would often go to this hiding spot to check on her prize when nobody was around to catch her.

One day, she noticed strange wet marks just under the baby's eyes. She was startled to see a tiny drop of water form and roll down its cheek. She watched breathlessly to see if it would happen again, but no further tears appeared.

Wooden babies don't cry, she assured herself. Surely an old pipe in the crawl space had leaked onto it. She hid her prize away once more and put it out of her mind.

A few nights later, Jessica awoke to muffled sobs coming from her closet. She found the baby and listened carefully to its little wooden lips. It was unmistakably crying low soft whines.

This troubled her deeply. If her mother heard this, she would find the manger baby and punish her. Jessica took an old silk scarf and wrapped it tight over the baby's mouth, silencing it. She placed the baby back in its hiding spot, shut the closet door, and enjoyed the peace and quiet.

The following night, Jessica heard scratching within the walls. Just mice, she decided. But when the scratching continued, she checked on baby Jesus and found that his hands had moved. His palms were open, and there was grit under his little wooden finger nails. Jessica wrapped him up in an old quilt and bound it with rope. There would be no way a baby could get out of this, she decided, and that would be that.

The next night, there was a tapping at Jessica's bedroom window. Jessica saw no one outside, but she opened the window to have a better look. As soon as she opened it, the Devil climbed through and introduced himself. "I'm very pleased with everything that you've done, Jessica!" the Devil proclaimed. "I've come to take this troublesome baby away from you."

Jessica was terrified. She knew the Devil was dangerous, and did not want to displease him. She fetched the wooden baby bound in the quilt, and held it out to him, arms trembling.

"Very good work indeed!" The Devil smiled as he accepted her offering. "You are quite dependable. I will be sure to call on you again and again!" The Devil climbed out the window and took the wooden baby away.

THE CANDY CANE

Father Whalen was rushing home from midnight mass in the bitter cold when he came upon a small child huddled next to the dumpster in the alley. The boy was bundled up in a black overcoat with red mittens, a dark green hat, and a yellow and red striped scarf. He puffed clouds of steam from beneath his scarf and stared intently at the brick wall before him. Father Whalen stooped down and asked, "Are you well, my child?"

The boy shook his head.

"Do you have parents?"

He shook it again.

Father Whalen worked with the homeless in the city, and it troubled him that more and more children were ending up on the streets. Luckily for this boy, Father Whalen had gone to tremendous lengths to feed and clothe the homeless. He was revered and respected throughout the community and had won many public service awards. Father Whalen knew the church shelter was operating tonight, and they would be happy to take the boy. But that was a mile in the opposite direction, and Father Whalen's warm comfortable home was just a few blocks away. It was late, and he was tired. Surely this cold dirty orphan would be more comfortable in his home, a far greater act of charity on Christmas Eve.

"Would you like to come home with me?" Father Whalen asked, taking the boy by the mitten.

The child nodded and they traveled hand in hand to Father Whalen's house. Once they arrived, Father Whalen removed his own coat, hat, and gloves and prepared a roaring fire he was sure the boy would remember for years to come. The boy watched curiously from the front door, still bundled up from head to toe.

"Have a seat by the fire," Father Whalen instructed. "I don't have much to offer you to eat, but you may have a candy cane off the Christmas tree, and I'll boil some hot water for tea."

The child hesitated by the door. Such a large comfortable room must be intimidating for him, Father Whalen decided. "Do you speak?"

The boy shook his head.

"But you do understand me, correct?"

The boy nodded.

"Then please, let's remove your coat and warm you up." Father Whalen helped the boy take off his coat, revealing a tattered old sweater covered in dark brownish red stains. They would have to do better than that! The child would be thrilled to have one of his old sweatshirts to sleep in. He helped the boy remove his gloves and was startled to find coarse dirty little hands with long sharp yellow finger nails. He would give this boy a bath and trim his hands and feet. By the time Father Whalen was done fixing him up, nobody would believe he had been a street urchin just a day earlier! Finally, he removed the boy's scarf and hat and nearly gasped at the child's wiry thinning hair and blemished face. The boy smiled at Father Whalen, revealing a mouth full of sharp rotting teeth.

"Oh my goodness." Father Whalen composed himself and led the boy over to the big leather armchair by the fireplace. He presented the boy with a candy cane and patted him on his scaly pink scalp. "I'm not sure that Santa Claus knows you're here tonight, but perhaps if you're good there will be a present for you at the church tomorrow." He smiled uneasily at the boy who stared vacantly back as he sucked the bottom of his candy cane.

Father Whalen excused himself to the kitchen to put on a pot of tea, wondering if perhaps the boy would be better off at a hospital. He peered into the living room through the crack in the kitchen door and observed the boy sucking away, glaring vacantly into the fireplace. The wounds on his face appeared to be infected. There was a cold unresponsive look in his eyes and a terrible rotting odor that was not typical of a street boy. He was quite hideous, but if he were to call an ambulance, Father Whalen would not have the chance to clean the child and present him to his congregation Christmas morning. No. Father Whalen would make an example through his good works. After Christmas mass, he would have the boy taken to the hospital and let the county deal with him.

He returned to the living room. "Have you heard the story of the baby Jesus?" he asked the boy as he sat across from him and reached for the Bible on the coffee table.

The boy shook his head and pulled the candy cane from his mouth revealing a thin white bottom. All the red lines had been sucked off.

"Would you like me to read to you?"

The boy shook his head.

Father Whalen laughed. "Come now, you'll enjoy this. And what chance does a dirty young boy have without the scripture?" The tea kettle in the kitchen gave a long shrill whistle. "I'll be right back," Father Whalen said.

The boy removed his candy cane again as if in response, revealing a thinner pointier bottom, like a white crayon. He held that pose, staring past Father Whalen with dead eyes.

Father Whalen smiled nervously and left to fetch the tea. He poured himself and the boy each a cup and was sure to give himself plenty of cream and sugar, but the boy would only need hot tea to lull him into a warm comfortable sleep. Sugar would only keep him awake.

He stooped down beside the boy and placed their tea on the side table. "Aren't you fortunate that God brought me to you tonight? You'll sleep soundly under my roof, child. Consider it my gift to you."

The boy removed his candy cane again. The bottom was now as sharp and pointy as a knitting needle.

Father Whalen laughed smugly to himself. "But that's the life of a priest I suppose. Give and give and give. A shame you have nothing to offer me in return."

The child smiled his dirty yellow smile and shoved the candy cane into Father Whalen's eye.

THE SNOWMAN

Pete, Michael, and Teddy entered the snowman building contest at school. All the other groups had brought hats, scarves, coal, carrots, buttons, and old mittens. The other children constructed beautiful perfect globes of pristine white snow from the front lawn of the school. There was a clown snowman, a police snowman, and many other attractive traditional snowmen decked out in warm colorful winter clothes with happy faces.

Pete, Michael, and Teddy however, had arrived an hour late having nothing with which to dress or decorate their snowman. Mr. Robins sneered at them as they tried to scrounge up enough snow to build a base. "I recommend using some of the snow at the curb boys." Mr. Robins pointed sharply to a pile of dirty gray slush that had been plowed to one side of the street. Mr. Robins was always picking on Pete in class for not paying attention. He had never liked Pete or his friends. Pete decided that if Mr. Robins thought it was so hilarious for them to use dirty snow, they would just go right ahead and make the dirtiest, nastiest, meanest snowman they could!

Pete rolled three big gritty boulders of street snow and stacked them while Michael rummaged in the dumpster behind the school. Teddy found two broken halves of a wet splintery plank, each full of bent nails, and jammed them in for arms. Michael found old beer bottle caps for buttons and shards of triangular green glass to make a serrated smile. Dirty brown leaves from the gutter became a mustache, and the sharp rusted metal bottoms of two old soup cans became enormous eyes.

20

Pete took a tattered old gray tweed cap from one of the other kids, but still something was missing. Michael searched the gutter by the curb and found the butt of an old cigar. He placed it firmly between the pointy glass teeth, and their twisted snarling snowman was complete.

Mr. Robins scoffed at the hideous snowman and only gave prizes to the cleanest, most traditional entries. He scolded the boys in front of everyone. "You've missed the point of this contest, gentlemen: to make a snowman everyone can enjoy." The other children laughed, and the boys went home angry.

The following morning all the other snowmen had been demolished. Hats, scarves, buttons and broken corncob pipes were strewn everywhere. Heads were severed and once strong snowmen had been crushed into messy piles. The only snowman left standing was Pete, Michael, and Teddy's filth encrusted creation. Their snowman stood dirty and tall, grinning its glassy grin. Everyone blamed the boys since their snowman had been the only survivor. Mr. Robins gave all three of them detention; he ordered them to destroy their snowman, clean up the school lawn, and apologize to their classmates. Each boy agreed to the punishment assuming that one of the other two had been responsible for the crime, but as they worked, they learned that none of them had done it. The injustice of it made them furious, and they agreed that their snowman should be protected. They carefully moved the snowman to the woods where he would be safe.

The following day someone had broken into Mr. Robins's classroom, overturned desks, strewn paper everywhere, splattered paint on the walls, and scratched up the blackboard. A series of dirty wet puddles led down the hall. Once again Pete, Michael, and Teddy's desks and lockers were left untouched. Mr. Robins again blamed the boys. This time they denied their guilt, but it was no use. The boys were suspended from school for the remainder of the week, and their parents grounded them until further notice. Pete was furious that nobody believed them. He wished that whoever was committing the crimes would keep doing it. Mr. Robins deserved it, and if this kept happening while the boys were grounded, it would prove their innocence.

The next morning at dawn, Pete awoke when a snowball broke through his bedroom window. Pete rushed to the window but found nobody. He picked up the snowball which crumbled in his hand revealing hundreds of dollars packed inside. He smiled as he imagined all the things he could buy. But his parents quickly entered his room and found him with the money. They saw the broken window and the snow on the ground and assumed Pete had snuck out. Michael and Teddy had awoken to snowballs through their windows as well, Michael's containing a gold watch and Teddy's a pair of rare silver coins. All of these items had been stolen from Mr. Robins's home. The boys were now in even more trouble and were facing expulsion.

After meeting with their parents, Mr. Robins, a police officer, and the school principal, the boys had a few minutes alone outside the principal's office. Pete knew the snowman had something to do with the crimes, and Michael agreed. Teddy was pale and silent at first, but finally admitted to having seen the snowman outside his house that morning. The boys agreed that they would have to sneak out after midnight and stop the snowman before it did something worse.

The boys met up that night, just outside the woods, and Michael found a dark red trail in the snow. They hurried to the spot where they had moved the snowman, but were too late. Mr. Robins lay still, face down in the snow at the foot of the snowman. The snowman dipped his spiked plank arm in the red snow underneath Mr. Robins and splattered blood over the boys' clothes in one swift motion. The snowman's glass teeth glinted, reflecting the bright orange embers of his lit cigar.

OPEN FIRE

Jack Heart and his eight-year-old son Jimmy awoke before sunrise the day after Thanksgiving to find a Christmas tree. They scoured the forest by the family cabin until they came across a sturdy eight-foot-tall pine, capped in snow and thick with dark green branches. Jack hacked away at the bottom of the trunk with his trusty axe, and little Jimmy took over at intervals until they had made a deep wedge-shaped notch. Then Jack pushed against the tree and snapped the base with a loud crack, shoving it onto the forest floor. They brushed away the snow, bundled their tree with canvas cloth and rope, and proceeded to pull it over the hill towards home.

As they dragged the tree behind them, Jimmy noticed something poking out of the snow in the path it had made. In front of the stump was a small rectangular stone with the inscription, "In loving memory." Jack felt terrible. He hadn't realized the tree had been planted in remembrance. But what could he do now? It was already chopped down, and his family would need a Christmas tree to decorate. He assured Jimmy the stone was nothing, and they continued home.

Jack's wife Mary adored the tree for its perfect height and shape, and its strong full branches. She rejoiced that the needles were firm and barely shed at all. She had already measured the perfect space for it in the living room and rearranged the furniture, so that the tree would stand proudly to the right of the fireplace. Their ten-year-old daughter Mina had already begun fighting with Jimmy over who would get to place the star on top. The family spent the entire day listening to holiday music, drinking hot apple cider, and meticulously adorning every branch with tinsel, ornaments, lights, beads, ribbons, and bows. By the end of the day, it was the most colorful, elegant Christmas tree the Hearts had ever assembled.

That very evening the trouble began. At 1:30AM Jack and Mary were awoken by Jimmy who claimed that the house was on fire. Jack smelled no smoke, nor could he find any flames. But Jimmy insisted that he had gotten up for a drink of water, and the living room was glowing like fire. Jack had built a roaring fire earlier that night, but it had died down long before he had gone to bed. Jack and Mary assured their son he had been dreaming and put him back to sleep.

On December 1st, Mina told her parents that the radio in her bedroom had been turning on by itself, and that the dial had been moving on its own. Jack could find nothing wrong with the radio, but he removed it from her bedroom to put her at ease.

That first week of December, Mary began to experience strange pranks. While using a jar of preserves or a bottle of ketchup in the kitchen, she would turn briefly and find it was suddenly missing. She would search everywhere, become incredibly irritated, and even blame the children who claimed to know nothing. Finally, the object would return in plain sight just as unexpectedly as it had vanished.

On December 9th, Jack returned from an errand one afternoon to find Mary comforting young Jimmy. Jimmy was in tears, terrified of an angry man who had come into his room to yell at him while he was playing alone. Jack searched the house, the grounds, and the woods while Mary contacted the Sheriff's Department. But they found no one. Jimmy told his parents later that the man was a ghost and came out of the fireplace.

After this, Jack and Mary became deeply concerned. The strange events continued throughout December. Jimmy

frequently claimed to see the Christmas tree light on fire, but nothing was burned. Mina became terrified to shut the bathroom door because of something that breathed into her ear when she was alone in there. Mary continued to lose items unexpectedly, and rediscover them in strange places. A hairbrush under the sink. A necklace in the fireplace. Paintings and pictures hung backwards and upside down. Jimmy, who had always been the enthusiastic youngest, had become quiet and withdrawn. He regularly claimed to see the "angry man" at night and soon began sleeping in his parents' bedroom.

It seemed that Jack was the only member of the family who had not encountered the strange phenomena directly, but he became increasingly nervous about the stone marker in front of the tree they had chopped down. He asked people in town if they knew anything about a memorial tree planted in the woods. Many of his neighbors claimed ignorance. A few reacted uncomfortably, but refused to elaborate or explain themselves. One very old woman claimed to remember that a young boy had died in a forest fire, and it had driven his father mad with grief. But the town records and library held no further clues.

The Sunday before Christmas, Jimmy again was terrorized by the "angry man," who he described as tall and thin with a red beard and fiery eyes. Jack had reached his limit. He quietly and calmly asked Mary to take the children to the car. Once he was alone in the house, he shouted to the entity to leave his family alone until his voice was hoarse. He then waited anxiously in the silent stillness of the living room, eyeing the fireplace and the Christmas tree suspiciously. But nothing happened. He joined his family in the car and treated them to a day of shopping in town.

When they returned, the Christmas decorations had been torn from the tree and strewn across the living room. Ornaments had been crushed, beads scattered, ribbons torn, and bulbs shattered. A fire blazed in the fireplace, spewing smoke and embers up the chimney, reaching unusually high with violent licks of bright flame. Jack searched the house, but there was no sign of broken entry, and there were no tracks leading to or from their home in the snow. Jack spent the entire evening cleaning the mess; but as soon as he finished, a vase exploded all by itself. He challenged the angry man to show himself but found nothing.

That evening the family awoke to the screams of Mina who had seen blazing balls of light in her bedroom. Both children began to suffer horrible nightmares and the entire family was now sleeping in the master bedroom. Mary made plans for the family to spend Christmas with her mother. But Jack refused to be driven out of his own home. Still, every time he confronted the entity it would terrorize his family even more. Finally, Jack and Mary called the local pastor.

The pastor toured the Hearts' cabin and interviewed each family member. He concluded that an evil spirit had entered their home and attached itself to Jimmy. Mina stayed with her grandmother on Christmas Eve while Jimmy, Jack, and Mary remained behind as the pastor prayed with them and blessed every room in the cabin. Throughout the process, Jimmy grew pale and distant; when they blessed the living room he became fixated on the fireplace. Jack stared deeply into the fireplace as well, determined to discover what Jimmy was so focused on. As he listened intently to the pastor's words, he found a pair of furious red eyes staring back at him.

Once the pastor had finished, Mary took Jimmy over to her mother's. When Jack saw them off, he noticed the color had returned to his son's face, and while he seemed tired and worn, Jimmy smiled and waved goodbye. The pastor warned Jack that these things were not so easily solved, and while their prayers might relieve the situation, the spirit could return in an even nastier form. Jack thanked the pastor and wished him a merry Christmas. Once he was alone in their house again, he knew what must be done.

He dragged the tree outside and pulled it through the snow, back into the woods. He found the stump and uncovered the memorial stone. He then rested the tree on its side on the spot where he had chopped it down. Jack collapsed in the snow and stared up into the star-filled sky, breathing a sigh of relief. He wasn't sure how, but he knew now that he'd removed the tree from his home, the entity would not bother his family again.

After some time, he pulled himself to his feet and trudged back up the hill. But he stopped suddenly in his tracks when he noticed the noxious stench of burning sulfur. A pillar of gray smoke slowly spread upwards into the air behind the white hill.

He struggled to the peak, gasping for breath, clutching his side. But he was too late. The family cabin was engulfed in flames.

The angry man emerged from the flickering wall of yellow and orange behind the front door. From the top of the hill, Jack heard the spirit's hateful laughter as he disappeared in the smoke.

THE FROZEN MITTEN

Will and his sister Sarah were playing in the woods behind their home when Sarah discovered a blue mitten, half buried in snow. Sarah tried to put in on, but it had become stiff and flat in the cold winter air. "Who do you suppose lost their mitten?" She asked her brother.

"Whoever they are, they're gone," Will decided, snatching the mitten away.

"But suppose they come looking for it? Suppose they're cold and they need it?"

"They won't," Will said. "Even if they could find it, it's no good now. It's frozen solid."

"We could take it home and wash and dry it," Sarah suggested.

"No," Will replied. "What good is one mitten without the other?" Will took the mitten and tossed it into the river.

The next morning, Sarah came to Will and told him about a terrible dream she had in which a cold, lost little girl searched for her mitten in the forest. Her hand froze as she wandered through the trees, unable to find her home. Will chastised his sister. The girl in the dream was not real, and Sarah had no reason to worry about her.

The following night, Sarah had yet another nightmare about the lost girl, huddled up against an old oak tree, shivering with her hand pulled up her sleeve. In the morning, she begged Will to return to the spot where they'd found the frozen mitten and leave one of theirs behind to replace it.

"Don't be stupid," Will said. "We need our mittens for

ourselves."

That night Will awoke in his bed to a terrible chill. The window in his bedroom had been opened somehow, and a cold breeze whistled through his room. The hot steam of his breath rose up into the air in small puffy clouds as he shivered under his covers.

The figure of a pale young girl appeared at the foot of his bed. Her lips were blue and trembling. She wore a gray knit cap and a long white coat. On one hand she wore a blue mitten. The other hand was pulled up her sleeve. She floated along the side of Will's bed, her eyes frozen and sad, snaky white vapor streaming from her lips.

"Please," she begged. "I'm lost and sick. Would you hold my hand and warm me up?" The girl reached to him, and a bluish white hand emerged from her sleeve, dead black finger tips outstretched. Her icy grip squeezed his hand.

Will screamed.

WASSAIL

Mr. and Mrs. Scotch waited anxiously in their living room for the faint sound of sleigh bells in the distance.

"Goodness!" Mrs. Scotch exclaimed. "Here come some more!" She fluttered to the window and pulled back the curtains. "They're coming right down the block, dear! Gee!"

"Now, now," Mr. Scotch replied with a soft laugh, "Take it easy, take it easy." He limped into the kitchen chuckling. "How many this time?"

"There are five of them!" Mrs. Scotch squealed. "Two women, a man, a little girl, and a little boy!"

"Oh, a lively bunch. Heh heh." From a tall metal thermos, Mr. Scotch poured hot apple cider into five ceramic mugs.

"They're coming!" Mrs. Scotch sang, bouncing up and down as sugary lyrics drifted up the walkway. She danced to the door and yanked it wide open just in time for a new verse of "Silent Night" to resonate through their home. "Oh dear!" Mrs. Scotch shouted over the shrill happy voices. "Oh my! Silent Night! More carolers are here, dear!"

"Well then," Mr. Scotch emerged from the kitchen with a tray of steaming cider, "they'll need hot drinks to soothe those pipes!"

"Oh boy!" Mrs. Scotch handed each caroler a cup of cider. The guests each savored the steamy beverages as they exchanged warm pleasantries. Once they had finished, they graciously returned their mugs, wished the Scotches a merry Christmas, and rang their bells over to the next house. The Scotches waved farewell and shut the door as the cheerful holiday music died out in the distance.

"We're just about out of cider," Mr. Scotch warned. "Do you think there'll be more carolers tonight?"

"My gracious yes!" Mrs. Scotch insisted, "Heat up some more."

Mr. Scotch retrieved another pot of cider from the refrigerator and placed it on the stove. He sprinkled in some cinnamon and a little sugar.

"Don't spare the arsenic, dear," Mrs. Scotch reminded from the other room.

"That's right," Mr. Scotch joked, "forgetful old me." He emptied a small bottle of poison into the mixture; then stirred vigorously. "Next year should be a quiet relaxing Christmas at home. Won't that be nice, dear?"

"Oh it'll be swell!" Mrs. Scotch exclaimed. "Just wonderful!"

THE GREEN BOX

Every December, Rodney looked forward to visiting his Aunt Victoria. Aunt Victoria was incredibly wealthy. She treated Rodney to fancy clothes, wonderful toys, and delicious meals. Her home was enormous, and Rodney's guest bed was three times as large and comfortable as his bed at home. Rodney would stay with Aunt Victoria from Christmas until New Years and live like a prince until it was time to go back to school.

Aunt Victoria doted on Rodney to no end. She had no children of her own, and each year she cherished the two weeks with Rodney. He put on plays, accompanied her on long walks, and drew sketches which his aunt proudly displayed in ornate frames. They baked cookies, read stories, and sang at the piano.

On Rodney's seventh Christmas, he found a long narrow package bundled in dark green velvet and tied with bright silk ribbon. Rodney and his aunt's names were embroidered in gold stitching on the top of the gift. When Rodney asked if he could open it, Aunt Victoria explained, "This is a gift for both of us, though we won't be opening it this year. Someday."

The boy begged and pleaded with his aunt, but she was quite firm. Rodney was happy with his many other gifts, and so he tried to hide his disappointment as he placed the green present back under the tree.

The following Christmas, the green gift was still there. He asked again if he could open it, to which Aunt Victoria smiled

and shook her head. "This is a very wonderful gift. But you are not ready for it. When you're older, you may open it."

Every year Rodney would ask about the green box, and every year his aunt told him to leave it be. Rodney's curiosity about the gift had grown tremendously. Aunt Victoria's presents were so lavish and thoughtful; he wondered what could possibly be better? Some nights he would sneak out of bed and hold the green box. The temptation to open it was incredibly strong. But his love and respect for his aunt was much stronger, and in the end he could not betray her wishes.

As Rodney grew older, it became more difficult to visit his aunt. School, girlfriends, and jobs were always getting in the way. Still, he wrote to his aunt regularly and promised he would find the time to visit.

One December, Rodney's aunt took ill. He drove to her home and was shocked and saddened to find she had become weak, frail, and bedridden in her old age. Aunt Victoria's doctor explained that all they could do was make her comfortable for as long as possible. Rodney stayed with her for two weeks and took very good care of her. One evening, Aunt Victoria called him into her room.

"You have been a wonderful nephew and brought great joy into my life. Watching you grow up has been the most beautiful gift I have ever received. However, there is one final gift we can give each other." Aunt Victoria produced the green box from her bedside drawer and gave it to Rodney. "Please open this now."

Rodney had almost forgotten about the green present. His heart thumped as he slowly undid the ribbon and unfolded the velvet wrapping to reveal a white box. Inside the white box was a rolled up piece of yellowing parchment paper and a gold pen. He unrolled the parchment to find a long legal document. At the bottom of the document was Aunt Victoria's signature, and next to it a place for Rodney to sign. His aunt beamed with joy. "I don't understand," Rodney said. "What is this?"

"I have no children of my own Rodney, and I am even wealthier than you know. If you sign this, you will inherit my entire estate."

Rodney was overcome with emotion. He had never imagined such a luxurious life for himself. He signed without hesitation. "Thank you," he said. "But I thought this was a gift for both of us?"

"Oh it is," Aunt Victoria replied. "I'm very old and in tremendous pain. The doctor says nothing can be done, except my organs are so hearty I could live on for years."

"I want you to live for many years," Rodney replied. "I'll do everything to keep you with me!"

"Oh, no, no," Aunt Victoria said with a wry smile. "By signing that document, you have agreed to kill me and end my pain tonight."

LIKE SKELETON HANDS

Matt and his family lived deep in the North Woods. Every day Matt walked his younger brother Travis five miles to school. Matt loved to tease his little brother. He would run ahead and hide, leaving Travis lost and confused. At home, he hid Travis's toys and told stories about monsters that lived under the bed and down the bathtub drain. One evening, after dinner, Matt stole Travis's dessert. Matt's mother caught him in the act and scolded him.

"Be nice to your brother! Santa Claus is always watching you, and if you're bad he will leave a wooden plank for us to beat you with instead of presents!"

"That's not true," Matt's grandmother explained. "Santa never visits the North Woods. Not enough people live here. He only visits cities and towns."

"Mother, please!" Matt's mother snapped.

"But it's true," she continued. "Santa doesn't have time to visit one lonely old house in the forest."

"Then how do our presents get here?" Matt asked.

"Santa leaves them at the edge of the woods, and the trees pass them across the forest to the homes where they belong."

"Mother, enough!" Matt's mother scolded again. "Don't tell them that old tale. You'll frighten them!"

But Matt was not frightened. If Santa was not watching, he could be as naughty as he wished. He loved to make his brother cry, and if nobody was around to see it, he would still get Christmas presents. All December long, Matt tormented Travis to and from school. He pushed him, shoved him, put snow down his pants, and stole his book bag. Travis cried and screamed and threatened to tell their mother, but Matt could always convince him not to snitch.

"Santa doesn't bring presents to cry babies or tattletales," Matt explained. "If you tell on me, there will be a wooden plank for *you* instead." Travis always kept quiet after this. Matt was older and smarter after all.

One day while walking home from school, Matt stole his brother's knit cap and ran down the forest path. He hid behind a tall oak tree and snickered to himself while his brother cried and called for him. Suddenly, something pushed Matt over and scraped at the back of his coat. Matt screamed and scrambled to his feet. He ran as far and fast as he could. When he finally reached home, he noticed that the back of his coat had been shredded to ribbons. A wolf could be prowling the path to school, he thought; maybe a bear? The longer Matt examined the tears, the more he wondered. Five long thin strips ran from the collar down to the bottom. What animal would do that? And why hadn't he heard anything?

Fortunately, winter break had started, and he wouldn't have to worry about walking the path for a few weeks. Matt waited inside the front door. He decided not to tell his mother about the attack, because she would yell at him for leaving Travis behind. After many long minutes of watching the path outside the window, Travis finally appeared, red faced and angry.

"I guess bears don't like the taste of crybabies," Matt whispered into his brother's ear, "because one was just about to eat you on the way home today." Travis's eyes expanded with fear. "You're lucky I distracted it for you. Next time I might not be so nice."

That evening, Matt heard a loud scraping sound. The branch of an old tree was scratching against his bedroom window. The branch was long and gnarled, and ended in five bony pointed smaller branches that looked like a gaunt tapering hand. Like a skeleton's hand, moving steadily down the windowpane. Each time it reached the bottom of the glass, it pulled away, rose up in the wind, and scraped again, slowly and methodically. Matt cautiously approached the window, drew his curtains shut, and quickly leapt back into bed. He covered his head with his pillow and tried his best to ignore the scraping and sleep.

On Christmas Eve, Travis had colored pictures for their mother and grandmother, but Matt hid them under the fireplace logs, so that their mother would burn them unknowingly. Travis was devastated that his gifts could not be found and started to work on new pictures. But as soon as nobody was looking, Matt threw the crayons into the fire to watch them melt, one by one. Travis became irritated and cranky as he found himself with fewer and fewer colors to work with. Matt's mother put him to bed early.

That night, once everyone was asleep, Matt snuck out of bed to see if presents had arrived. As he crept into the living room, he saw that the window next to their Christmas tree was open. A long grayish-brown arm reached through the window and deposited bright shiny packages under the Christmas tree. It was a tree branch, with the same bony fingers that had scraped Matt's windowpane. It carefully placed each package forming little pyramids of gifts. Matt was both excited and afraid. His heart beat frantically as he watched the wooden talons fill the bottom of the Christmas tree with presents. Then it silently retreated out the living room window and shut it. Matt cautiously approached the window and peered out at the

treetops. He watched as the long thin branches of the forest moved back and forth, passing packages through the woods. One at a time, box by box. Their thin, claw-like boughs working in unison like a secret, silent dance.

Matt drew the curtains shut and turned his attention to the brightly wrapped gifts under the tree. He quietly examined the first one he saw. A silvery tag read "From Santa, to Travis." Matt reached for another present: "To Travis." He reached for another and another. All of the gifts the trees had brought were for Travis. There must have been some kind of mistake! Perhaps the trees would deliver his presents next. Santa had no idea Matt had been naughty, so why wouldn't he get presents? He didn't see any coal, or a wooden plank like his mother had warned him either. Matt reopened the curtains, expecting to see the trees hard at work, but their dance had ended.

Matt slumped back upstairs. He quietly shut the door to his bedroom and was about to go back to sleep when he heard a soft scrape on his windowpane. The same tree branch from the other night tapped with its long pointy skeleton finger. Matt approached slowly and saw that a nearby branch was holding a bright gold box tied with red ribbons. It held the gift up to the window, and Matt approached, pushing his face against the glass. The silvery tag read "To Matt."

He gasped with excitement. His presents were being delivered directly to his room! Matt hurried to open the window, but as soon as he did so, the sharp wooden talons snatched him up and carried him off into the darkness.

THE SMELL

Elane and her mother were thrilled that Elane's father would be home for the holidays. Her father was a traveling salesman and had worked hard to support his wife and daughter for many years. Now that Elane had graduated from college and her father could retire, their family would be whole all year round.

On Christmas Eve, he called them from the train and promised a very special holiday surprise. Elane and her mother prepared a big meal, wrapped gifts, and eagerly waited for her father to arrive. They played old Christmas records on the highest volume and danced with each other to pass the time. As soon as Elane's father was home, he would prepare a roaring fire; then they would enjoy a scrumptious dinner and exchange gifts.

By nine o'clock that evening, however, Elane's father had not arrived. By ten o'clock, still no sign. Her mother paced anxiously, certain that something had gone wrong. The train was scheduled to arrive at seven, and the cab ride home would only have taken ten minutes. Elane assured her that it was a simple delay and took a walk to the train station to prove that everything was fine.

When she arrived, she noticed several police cars and a crowd of distraught townspeople. She was horrified to learn that the bridge just outside of town had collapsed and the train derailed into the river. Many were dead, and more were missing. Elane returned home to her mother with the terrible news. Christmas came and went, but there was still no word on her father's fate. Elane's mother was wrought with grief. They both knew in their hearts her father was no longer with them.

No sooner than they accepted his fate… a terrible odor welcomed itself into their home. It was a nauseating, pungent, overpowering stench they could not escape. Elane searched everywhere: the basement, the cabinets, the refrigerator, the bathrooms, the attic, the crawlspace, the yard. But she could find no explanation for the foul smell. It eventually became so overbearing that it made Elane's mother ill. Elane moved her mother to a neighbor's house temporarily and hired a handyman to help determine what could be done.

The handyman quickly assessed that there was a hollow space under the floorboards. Sometimes animals make their way under there to die, he explained. Within a month, the body would decompose completely and her mother could move back into the home. It would simply be too expensive to tear up the floorboards and remove the carcass.

The young handyman noticed how tired and sad Elane was. She explained that her father had just passed, and the handyman was touched by her grief and impressed by her concern for her mother. Elane found great comfort in the handyman, and they began to date. Many months later, they married happily. The union brought great joy into Elane and her mother's lives, and by the following Christmas Elane was with child. Her husband prepared a roaring fire that year, and it felt to all that their family was whole once again.

As happy as she was, Elane still missed her father terribly. Her father had always told her that he would make sure she was loved, respected, and cared for before he left this life. Elane knew that her father would be happy that she had found a compassionate, loving husband. Her only wish was that he could return to meet him.

As she poked the logs in the fireplace, she heard a long scraping ruckus up the chimney. Elane shrieked as a big yellow skeleton stuffed in a tattered, worn, red Santa suit fell smack onto the fire and burned before her eyes. The skeleton's hands were clutching a sack full of presents. Around the wrist bones was her father's gold watch. It seemed that her father had gotten off one stop earlier to purchase gifts and give them the surprise of their lives.

THE DINNER GUEST

A young father passed away in late November, and the family buried him on the cemetery hill just outside their home. All December long, the man's daughter and son gazed out their bedroom window and watched the snow fall on his grave. Their mother told them that their father could watch over them from the peak of the hill. But the girl wondered why, if their father was so close, he could not come down to see them.

Every night after their mother tucked them in, the little girl prayed that their father would come back for Christmas. During the day, she encouraged her younger brother to kneel with her by the window, knowing that if they prayed their hardest, God would have to listen.

As Christmas drew nearer, the girl found her mother crying in the kitchen as she prepared sweets and baked goods. "Don't cry mother. Father is coming back soon," the little girl assured her. "We've prayed for it every night since he was buried!"

"Oh no, sweetheart," her mother explained, "God doesn't do things like that. No matter how hard you pray."

"But we've been very good," the girl protested. "And we love father so much."

"Yes dear, but no matter how hard you pray, God will never send your father back to us. It's not something he can do."

The girl was devastated. If God could not help them, all was lost. She fled to the top of the hill and sobbed over her father's grave.

"What's the matter, young lady?" An old grave digger had appeared behind her father's headstone. He was leaning on a rust encrusted shovel and bundled up in a gray coat and scarf. The steam of his breath floated out from behind the wrappings of his scarf which covered the lower part of his face, and his cold blue eyes gazed sympathetically into hers.

"I've prayed to God to bring back my father, but my mother says he won't do it," the girl sniffled.

"Oh my, no, no…" the old grave digger shook his head slowly. "God certainly doesn't do those kinds of things. That's the work of the Devil."

"But the Devil is evil," the girl said. "He would never help."

"Quite wrong." The grave digger held up his finger and tapped on the headstone. "He would bring people back all the time… if only their loved ones would bother to ask."

The girl stared curiously at her father's grave. When she looked back up again, the strange man had vanished. That night she thought long and hard about what he had said. Since God would not answer her prayers, she would have to pray to the Devil instead.

When she asked her brother to join her, he refused at first. He too knew the Devil was bad, but she insisted there was nobody else who could grant this wish. They both missed their father terribly, and before long the boy was pleading with the Devil as well. Both children prayed much harder than they had to God, begging the Devil to have their father home for Christmas, knowing that this would make their mother happy and their family complete once more.

On Christmas Eve, the children helped their mother prepare an enormous feast of roast turkey, mashed potatoes, corn on the cob, biscuits, and gravy. All day long the little girl snuck glances out the window at the top of the hill, but saw nothing save the steady snowfall. As they sat down to say grace, the girl stole one final look at the cemetery hill. Her heart leapt with joy when she saw a dark shadowy figure climbing out of the snow at the peak. The shadow slowly lumbered down the hill, limping and hobbling. Reaching out at tree stumps and fence posts for support as it made its way down through the snowdrifts and over the fence. The girl's mother was just about to scold her for staring out the window during grace, when the door thumped three times.

The children's mother answered the door and clutched at her heart as she gasped for breath. The man behind the door was pale and gaunt; his fingernails long and black and his gums pinkish white, with sharp pointy teeth. His mouth was pulled back revealing a clenched jaw, and his eyes were glassy, cupped by dark purple circles. But the features, while worn by decay, did not lie. He was her husband, dressed in his good Sunday suit, which was stained with dirt and dusted with snow.

Their mother fell to her knees and praised God's name. She held him and kissed him and asked a dozen questions. Their father stared blankly past his wife and eyed the feast on the table. "I'm hungry," he said with a weak gravelly voice. "I haven't eaten in so long, and I'm so very hungry."

"Yes of course dear!" She led him to his chair while the children fixed him generous portions of everything. Their father ferociously tore apart a drumstick and guzzled a pile of potatoes. He gorged on biscuits and vegetables, but all the while he shook his head and made a confused dissatisfied face. "More!" He growled.

The children fixed him another serving loaded with meat and gravy and he devoured it frantically, his knife and fork scraping at his plate in a frenzy--his little sharp teeth shredding and tearing. His throat gulping and sucking. He cleaned his plate again and groaned. "I'm still hungry..."

"But you've eaten so much," their mother said. "You're bound to feel full soon. Perhaps you ought to lie down?"

"I'm starving!" he shouted. He reached for another drumstick and tore into it like an animal, gnawing the bone for several minutes after he had stripped it clean. Finally, he tossed the bone aside and pounded on the table.

"Please dear," their mother sobbed, "lie down and rest!"

"I'm not tired!" he screamed. "I've been lying down for days!" He gave a terrible snarl as he yanked the tablecloth, knocking Christmas dinner all over the floor. Silverware clattered and dishes shattered. He pounded his fists and shrieked, "Why am I still hungry?!"

The children sobbed as their mother gently took their father in her arms and pleaded with him, "You're not well, please calm down."

He slowly settled down, breathing steady raspy breaths. He held his wife close to him. "I'm so hungry..." he whimpered.

"But you've eaten so much," she sobbed.

"I feel like I've eaten nothing. I'm going to starve...." He held their mother's neck close to him, and suddenly his eyes and jaw opened wide. "So... hungry," he whispered coarsely. His pointy canines extended into two long dagger-shaped fangs.

"It's going to be okay," their mother whispered soothingly. "You're back with your family, and we'll do anything to make you better."

"Good to know..." He snarled, as he sank his teeth into her neck and drank.

THE TRUNK IN THE ATTIC

Justin had heard from a friend at school that there was no Santa Claus. "All parents hide toys in the attic," the friend explained. "On Christmas Eve once you're asleep, they bring them downstairs." Justin did not believe it at first, but the longer he thought about it, the more curious he became.

The entrance to Justin's attic was just outside his bedroom. One simply tugged a cord and a stepladder pulled down from a panel in the ceiling. Justin had never been up there. Only his parents and grandfather were allowed.

"There are mice and spiders up there," his mother said when he asked. "Some of the floorboards are weak. It's unsafe, and I don't want you going up there."

"Are there toys?" Justin asked.

"Don't be silly," his mother replied. "There's nothing fun in the attic."

Justin told this to his friend at school who merely replied, "All parents are liars. There *are* toys up there. Trust me!"

Finally, Justin couldn't resist the temptation to check for himself. Late at night when his parents and grandfather were fast asleep, he crept out into the hallway and stood on a chair to pull the attic cord. The step ladder dropped with a dull thud. Justin waited to see if this would wake his parents, but it did not. He slowly ascended the steps, each one creaking loudly. Still

Justin's parents slept. He entered the dim, pale blue attic. Only moonlight flooded in through a small round window. The floor was dusty and gray. Cobwebs covered the rafters.

"Hello," came a coarse whisper from an old rocking chair in the corner. Justin's heart skipped a beat. A gaunt man concealed in shadows rocked silently. "May I ask what you're doing up here?"

"I'd heard there were toys up here," Justin said.

"Yes, there are…" the man pointed to a dusty old trunk. "That trunk contains the most wonderful toys you'll ever find. But you must first place something of value in it. Find something important, and bring it back here."

Justin quietly descended the attic steps and snuck carefully into his parents' bedroom as they slept. He found his mother's antique necklace. It had been passed down for many generations in her family, and Justin knew it was very important to her. He brought it upstairs and opened the trunk. The inside was empty.

"Place the necklace inside and shut the lid," the man in the rocking chair told him. Justin did as he was told. When he reopened the trunk, the necklace was gone and in its place he found the most incredible toy train carved from pinewood and hand painted, with silver wheels. When he pulled it backwards, it chugged along the floor all on its own. It was the most amazing toy train Justin had ever seen, and he played with it for hours in the attic until he felt very tired. Before he went back down to his bedroom, he attempted to put the train back in the trunk and retrieve his mother's necklace, but the necklace would not come back.

"You cannot get back what you gave," the man explained. "But you have something new now. And the more important the thing you give, the more wonderful the item you receive."

The next day Justin thought long and hard about what else he might get from the attic trunk. His mother was terribly distressed about her missing necklace, and Justin hid his new train so she wouldn't ask questions. He felt bad about the necklace, but the excitement of thinking about the trunk made him feel better. That night, once the adults in the house were asleep again, Justin snuck out of his room. He silently slipped into the bedroom of his sleeping grandfather. He carefully removed his grandfather's wooden leg and stealthily brought it up into the attic.

The man in the rocking chair congratulated him, "Very good! I myself am eager to see what that will bring you!" Justin placed the wooden leg in the trunk and shut it. When he reopened it, he found an incredible mechanical soldier made from wood and metal. When Justin wound him up, the soldier marched and fired tiny ball bearings from his little rifle! Just holding his soldier made Justin feel extremely happy. He played in the attic all night long until the man in the rocking chair reminded him that dawn was approaching. Justin quietly went back downstairs and closed the attic. He reluctantly hid his soldier with his train, although it was painful to be apart from it.

That day Justin's grandfather lamented that his leg was gone. Justin's parents were angry and confused. Justin denied knowing anything about the crime, and they all believed him because he was normally very good. It would be a long time before his grandfather's leg could be replaced, and he was sad to be using a rickety old wheelchair.

Justin felt bad at first, but then he would take out his train and his soldier and feel incredibly happy once more. Justin was lucky to be the only boy he knew with these wonderful toys, and he played with them every chance he got over the next few days. But soon Justin wondered what else the trunk had to offer. Something even more important than the wooden leg would surely be exchanged for something even more wonderful than the train and soldier which brought him so much joy. The possibility of an even greater toy made Justin exhilarated.

That night, Justin crept out again after everyone was asleep to fetch his father's yellow canary from his study. He grasped the bird firmly as he snatched it from its gilded cage and held its beak shut between his fingers, so that it would not wake his parents. He brought it up to the attic with him, and the man in the rocking chair became overjoyed.

"Yes! That will bring you something truly spectacular!" the man said. Justin sealed the bird in the trunk and listened as its muffled frantic chirps came to an abrupt halt. Justin tingled with excitement as he reopened the trunk. Inside was a shimmering chrome space helmet with a glinting gold lightning bolt above a glass visor. His hands shook as he placed it over his head. When he wore the helmet, he could actually see the vast expanse of outer space. The sun, the moon, the planets, and every star stretched out in in front of him. The helmet made him feel like he was flying faster than the speed of light. The incredible weightlessness brought far greater joy than the other toys.

When he heard the man in the rocking chair tell him the sun was rising, he had to force himself to tear the space helmet off his head. He felt tremendous disappointment when he saw the old dusty attic again, and the pink glow of sunrise in the small circular window. He would put it back on as soon as he could.

Justin's father was devastated that his canary was gone because he had cared for it for many years. Again, Justin's parents asked him if he had anything to confess, which made him furious. He couldn't believe they would think him capable of such crimes, after having been so good for so long. He screamed at his parents and cried at their accusations until they believed his innocence once more.

Every quiet moment Justin had to himself, he would close his bedroom door and wear his space helmet. He began to truly hate church, and school, and dinnertime for taking him away from the wonderful feeling of weightlessness. He slept very little and wore the helmet as much as he possibly could.

But as much as he loved the helmet, over the next few weeks he found himself thinking again about the trunk in the attic. He knew there had to be something even better to be had.

One night, he crept up into the attic and begged the man in the rocking chair for advice, "I've given my mother's necklace, my grandfather's wooden leg, and my father's canary. But I know there are even better toys!" He begged, "Please, what else can I give that would be even *more* important?!"

"I'm glad you asked," the shadowy man said as his rocker came to a stop. "Step over here, son."

Justin approached him, and the man held up a blood and rust crusted old hacksaw. "If you place your left hand in the trunk, you will have a toy more fantastic than anything you could ever imagine."

Justin closed his eyes, took a deep breath, and held out his left hand.

THE MANIAC

Kathy Nelson was spending Christmas Eve with her three young daughters. The girls were ecstatic about Santa Claus, and Kathy had spent hours calming them down and putting them to sleep. It was an exhausting task; one that was always easier with her husband's help. But he had agreed to work the graveyard shift to get double overtime for the holidays. They had struggled to make ends meet this year, so the extra money would help. Still, Kathy felt sorry for her poor husband working on Christmas Eve, so she planned to wait up and surprise him with a little holiday romance. She slipped into a soft robe and put a bottle of wine on ice. Then she relaxed and warmed her feet by the fireplace in the living room.

It would be a few hours before her husband's shift ended, so she turned on the TV to kill time. The words "Kane County Psychiatric Hospital" flashed across the screen, and she increased the volume.

"--the murder of two doctors and an armed security guard. This patient is considered extremely dangerous. Police are asking that any suspicious behavior be reported. As a precaution, all residents in the vicinity are encouraged to lock their doors and windows. Do not under any circumstances stop for hitchhikers."

Kathy's heart pounded as the news unfolded. The hospital was only a few miles down the road. Her friend Gale worked there. They showed a picture of the escaped patient; he had a long lank gray beard and a sloping brow. His mouth twisted into a sneer full of crooked yellow teeth. Kathy took a deep breath;

then calmly double bolted the front door. She checked all the windows in the kitchen, the living room, and the dining room. Then she proceeded upstairs to secure the bedrooms.

A sharp tug at her robe in the dark hallway caused Kathy to cry out. She spun around to find her youngest daughter. "Mommy, can I have some water?"

"Yes, yes, of course dear. Then straight back to bed."

"Is Santa here yet?"

"No sweetheart, he won't come until you're fast asleep." Kathy got her daughter a glass of water and escorted her back to bed. Her older sisters slept peacefully. She kissed her youngest on the forehead and locked the three windows as she scoured the backyard for anything unusual. Nothing but pristine white snow and the narrow branches of stark trees swaying in the wind.

Kathy proceeded to lock the remaining upstairs windows, then returned downstairs. She turned on every light she could as she moved through the house. She knew that if she acted like her husband was home and all was well, a criminal was less likely to break in. She turned the TV back on, but the special report was over. She tried the other channels, but nobody was reporting on the escaped man. It was well after midnight by now, and her husband would not be home any time soon. Just as she reached for the phone to call him, it rang shrilly in her hand. The display showed a number she did not recognize. She answered, "Hello?"

For a moment there was only heavy breathing, then a choked sob, "Kathy?"

Kathy breathed a sigh of relief. It was her friend Gale from the hospital. "Are you all right?" Kathy asked.

"I'm fine, I wasn't working tonight. But I want you to listen to me. I'm calling everyone I know in the area. The man who escaped stole a coat from the children's ward. A red and white Santa Claus coat. Draw the curtains, lock all the doors and windows, and turn off all the lights. This man isn't interested in stealing from you. He's looking for victims. If he doesn't think you're home, he'll move on to the next house."

She thanked Gale quickly and hung up. She raced through the house, turning all the lights back off again. She turned off the TV as well. She remembered her husband's shotgun, locked away in the back of their bedroom closet. He had shown her how to load it in case of an intruder.

"Mommy?" Kathy's youngest appeared at the top of the stairs again. "Is Santa here?"

"No, not yet sweetie. Go to bed."

"But I heard someone moving around very fast."

"That was me, sweetheart."

"But I saw him in the backyard, and then I heard someone moving in the hallway."

Kathy's blood curdled. "You saw Santa... in the backyard?"

"Yes."

Kathy raced upstairs to her daughters' bedroom. The two older girls slept deeply; her youngest drifted in behind her. Kathy peered out the window into the yard and saw big bold impressions in the snow. Boot prints winding back and forth, leading in and out of the yard. Kathy took a deep breath. All of the downstairs curtains were drawn wide open. The kitchen light was still on, and she had left the phone in the living room. "Sweetheart?" she asked her daughter calmly. "When you looked down at Santa Claus, did he look back up at you?"

"I don't know Mommy. It's very dark outside."

"I want you to go back to bed. He won't leave you presents if you're up and about. Stay in bed, under the covers and go to sleep." Kathy drew the curtains shut on all the girls' windows. She kissed her youngest goodnight and shut their door tight. She proceeded to her own bedroom and retrieved the shotgun from the locked drawer in the closet. She calmly and carefully loaded it, then slowly crept down the stairs. She saw nothing outside the living room window as she silently moved towards the phone, weapon in hand. Suddenly there was a loud crash from below. The basement! She had neglected to check the basement windows!

Kathy rushed to the kitchen and quickly dead-bolted the basement door as strong legs lumbered up the wooden steps. The man bashed and beat the door from the other side, but it held securely. Kathy took a few steps back and aimed her shotgun. "Go away! Leave us alone!" she shouted. "The police are on their way right now!"

The man behind the door groaned and wheezed, then laughed to himself and thumped back down the stairs. She waited breathlessly for a few minutes and then decided that even if she did alert the police, they would never arrive in time. She was going to take care of this problem herself. The man in the basement didn't know she was armed. She should have just let him come, so she could surprise him. She slowly unbolted the door, and kicked it open. The wooden stairs led into the dark shadowy cellar.

"I'm up here!" She shouted. "Come up and get me. I'm all alone."

She pointed the barrel of her shotgun down into the shadows, but nothing stirred. She cautiously descended. "You can come out now," she whispered, her voice trembling. But the basement appeared to be empty. Only little drifts of powdery snow wafting in through an open window. The man must have left.

She turned and raced back up to the kitchen. He was going to try and get in another way. She locked the basement door again and walked towards the living room. She drew each set of curtains shut as she passed them. When she reached the front door, she peered outside... and saw him.

He strode up the walkway in his big red coat; the white tassel of his Santa hat bouncing as he confidently approached the door. Kathy undid the lock. She had a perfect shot lined up. The man would never see it coming. She pulled the door open, aimed, and fired in one fluid motion, blasting the man in the knee. He fell over and screamed in agony. Kathy laughed, shouted, and breathed deep sighs of relief.

"Mommy!" her daughter called from upstairs. "I heard something. Is Santa here?"

"Go back to bed!" Kathy cried. "Go back to bed and shut that door tight!"

"Kathy!" came an anguished voice from down the front walkway. "Kathy... what's happening?"

She gasped and raced outside. The man pulled down his white Santa beard and groaned in agony. "Kathy... why???" It was her husband! She rushed to his side and held him. His leg was badly wounded. The snow around him was sprinkled with bright red dots.

"I'm so sorry. I didn't know it was you. I... why are you dressed like this?!"

"I got off early to surprise the girls..."

"Lie still." Kathy turned to call an ambulance; then froze in her tracks. Standing in the open door frame was the escaped man, dressed in his big red and white coat, grinning with his crooked yellow teeth and waving with a black gloved hand. He took a step backwards inside the house, slammed the door, and locked it.

SOMETHING IN THE BASEMENT

Jeremy was excited to be staying with a new foster family for the holidays. When he arrived, his new parents and brother greeted him in front of a white two story home, blanketed in snow and lined with glowing colored lights. The brick walkway was shoveled neatly and a freshly built snowman held a poster board sign that read "Welcome Jeremy!"

His new foster father shook his hand. "Welcome to your new home Jeremy. We are Mr. and Mrs. Craft. This is our son Steven."

Mrs. Craft kissed Jeremy on the cheek and hugged him tight. "Absolutely anything you need you just let us know. This is your home now, and we're so happy that you're here with us!"

Steven took Jeremy's bags, and the family showed him around the house. The home was modest, but well kept. Each room was immaculate. There was a cozy little kitchen, a dining room, a quaint parlor which housed a brightly colored Christmas tree, and two little upstairs bedrooms. The family took Jeremy back downstairs to the kitchen where they all had hot chocolate and freshly baked chocolate chip cookies. "It warms our hearts to have you." Mrs. Craft beamed. "You know Steven always wanted a brother. But Mr. Craft and I couldn't have any other children."

"You two are going to get along just great," Mr. Craft said. "We want you to feel right at home. Just help yourself to absolutely anything you need."

Mrs. Craft cleared her throat and smiled broadly at her husband.

"Oh yes," Mr. Craft said. "Except the basement. Never ever go into the basement." He gestured to a simple white door on the far side of the kitchen.

"Why can't I go down there?" Jeremy asked.

Mrs. Craft laughed politely and tossed her arms up in the air as she shrugged. "Well Jeremy, it's simply not allowed. We don't go down there… ever."

"Sometimes Mrs. Craft and I go down there to get things done."

"Oh yes, the laundry and such." Mrs. Craft smiled and nodded. "And sometimes if I'm very very busy I might ask Steven to run down and grab something for me."

"But never go down there, no matter what." Mr. Craft patted Jeremy on the shoulder and smiled. "We're so happy to have you here," he added.

Jeremy smiled politely and nodded. He wasn't sure what could be so off-limits in the basement, but he was grateful for his new foster family and happy to respect their rules.

His first night in Steven's room, Jeremy heard strange noises in the walls. A slurping sticky sound that came from the vent behind his bed. Every time Jeremy started to nod off, the slurping would start again. Eventually, the slow steady slurps were joined by a series of loud metallic bangs. Jeremy lay awake all night. He whispered to Steven, but his foster brother slept soundly through it all. In the morning, Jeremy asked Steven if he had heard the noises.

"Oh that's nothing," Steven said. "That's just noises."

"What's making the noises?" Jeremy asked.

"Houses make noises at night," Steven explained. "That's just noises in the vent. I'm used to them and you'll get used to them too."

Jeremy tried his best to ignore the strange noises, but every night he listened intently to the sucking slurping sound behind his bed and the loud unpredictable bangs and bumps in the vents. It didn't sound like the squeaking thumping sounds of a heater. It sounded wet and angry.

One afternoon, while Jeremy and Steven were eating lunch in the kitchen, they heard the buzzer go off on the dryer in the basement.

"Mom!" Steven called. "You want me to change the wash loads?!"

"No sir!" Mrs. Craft shouted from the other room. She glided into the kitchen and blocked the basement door with her smiling face. "I'll get it sweetheart." She opened the basement door only slightly and slipped through the narrow gap, shutting it behind her. Jeremy listened closely as Mrs. Craft's footfalls creaked down the basement steps, and the hinged door of a metal dryer opened. For a good long while there was only silence, and Jeremy turned back to his lunch.

But suddenly there came a loud series of powerful thuds. Mrs. Craft shouted inaudibly, and a steady stream of whooshes and cracks interplayed between the thumps and crashes. Mrs. Craft let out an angry shriek unlike anything Jeremy had heard from her before. Then he just barely made out the words, "Shoo! Shoo! Enough!" Followed by her footsteps creaking back up the stairs. The door opened just enough for Mrs. Craft and a small white basket of laundry to emerge. She slammed it shut, then turned to Jeremy, a great big smile on her face as usual. Her hair was disheveled, her red lipstick smeared across her cheek, and there were strange pink circular marks running along her neck in two even rows. "Heavens to Betsy!" she exclaimed. "Can't a gal get a fresh load of laundry?!"

Jeremy stared, dumbfounded as she plopped her basket at the other end of the kitchen table and started folding. "Oh gosh!" she cried out holding up a torn piece of black cloth. She fished into the basket and removed more bits of shredded black fabric which Jeremy soon recognized as his favorite pullover. "Oh, I'm sorry honey!" She held the strands of torn material out to him. "Someone's a little too excited that there's a new smell in the house." She finished folding the clothes as Jeremy examined the remains of his sweatshirt. It smelled like rotting seafood. Mrs. Craft kissed Jeremy on the top of the head. "I think there just might be a new sweatshirt under the old tree for someone this Christmas." She smiled and winked at him as she took the clean laundry upstairs.

That night before bed, Jeremy begged Steven to tell him what exactly was in the basement. "Is there a dog down there? A big mean dog?"

"Nah!" Steven assured him. "There's no dog. But you're not supposed to go down there. Just don't go down there, and you'll be fine." Jeremy continued to hound him. Finally, Steven nodded and whispered, "There *is* something in the basement. But we can't get rid of it, so we just have to live with it."

"What is it?" Jeremy asked.

"Well… at first it was really small…" Steven trailed off.

"Lights out boys," Mr. Craft said from the doorway, silhouetted by the hall light. "No more talking. Go to bed."

That night a terrible odor crept over the bedroom, like week-old fish stew. And the horrible banging, sucking, squishing sounds continued. The next morning Jeremy overheard Mr. and Mrs. Craft arguing downstairs.

"I'm telling you that thing is becoming a real pain the behind!" Mrs. Craft sighed.

"Nothing to be done. If I get my promotion maybe we can move. But even so, I just don't know how to sell a house with a... thing like *that* in it. We'll just have to make do for now."

Mrs. Craft snapped, "It keeps. Getting. Bigger!"

"I know," he said. "Shhhh..."

"And now it smells a new person in the house, and it's all excited," she whispered. "And Jeremy's interested in the whole thing. You can just tell by the look on his face!"

"Well you shouldn't have insisted on a foster child!" Mr. Craft snapped.

"You said the thing was *dead*!" Mrs. Craft hissed.

"I thought it *was*!"

Jeremy wasn't sure what to do anymore. He wanted to find out what was in the basement, but he didn't want to cause trouble. Even Steven refused to tell him anything more. "My dad yelled at me for talking about it too much last night," he said simply. "Just don't go down there, and you'll be fine."

By dinnertime that evening, the whole house reeked of the horrible stench of rotting fish. All three members of the Craft family tried to hide their revulsion, but Jeremy could tell they smelled it too. Jeremy felt sick, and he couldn't bring himself to eat. Finally, Mrs. Craft put down her fork and smiled to her husband. "Would you be a lamb and check the basement for us?"

Mr. Craft made a grim face and nodded. He grabbed a meat cleaver off the kitchen counter and entered the basement, slamming the door behind him. He thumped violently down the stairs then shouted ferociously. There was a long series of bangs, scrapes, and crashes. Mr. Craft's muffled rage reverberated through the floor. Steven held his nose and stared down at his plate while Mrs. Craft smiled warmly at Jeremy. "Everything's fine sweetie," she assured him.

More banging, crunching, and a wet slopping splashing noise muffled through the simple white basement door, and Mr. Craft screamed a shrill angry cry of despair. Then there was a stiff empty silence. Mrs. Craft continued to smile. "Steven," she said finally. "Check and see if your father needs any help in the basement."

The color drew out of Steven's face and his eyes became as wide as two sand dollars.

"Steven," Mrs. Craft insisted, her stern smile persisting.

Steven prepared to pull his seat back from the table just as a slow steady series of thumps made their way up the basement stairs. Everyone stared as the knob turned and the basement door slowly creaked open. Mr. Craft emerged without his cleaver. His shirt was torn open, and his chest and neck were covered in the same even rows of pink circular marks that Jeremy had seen on Mrs. Craft the other day. Mr. Craft's arms and legs were stained with an inky black liquid, and there was a deep gash on his forehead that was oozing blood. "Well," he said. "I guess I'm going to have a hot shower and get to bed early."

"All right then, dear. We'll clean up these dishes."

"What is that black stuff?" Jeremy whispered.

"Oh those old leaky pipes in the basement..." Mr. Craft trailed off as he made his way upstairs. "You know how it is..."

That night the house was unusually quiet, and for the first time since he'd arrived, Jeremy fell into a deep sleep. But in the middle of the night, he awoke to the same foul stench of old fish. He opened his eyes and a chill ran down his back as he noticed a long thick black object coiled around his bed like a big shadowy snake. Jeremy shouted and frantically tried to get out of bed, but the big black snake tightened its grip and pinned him in place. He screamed and struggled as the dark tube coiled up around his neck and yanked the entire bed frame backwards, slamming it against the wall. The bed rose up and smashed violently back down. It shook back and forth, and side to side. The black snake tightened more and more, splintering the sides of the wooden bed frame and ripping the edges of the mattress open. Jeremy felt it sucking on his face, pulling at his skin.

"Hey! Hey!" Mr. Craft barged into the room. He kicked frantically behind Jeremy's bed until the snake released its grip, recoiling back into the wall. Jeremy screamed and ran out into the hallway.

Mrs. Craft grabbed him and held him tight, shushing him and stroking his hair. "It's all right now. You're fine. You're absolutely fine."

Jeremy sobbed. His whole body trembled.

"It's all right. You just had a nightmare," Mrs. Craft said. "You're fine."

"It wasn't a nightmare it was real!" Jeremy insisted. "What's down there?! What's in the basement?!"

"You were just... sleeping!" Mrs. Craft said sternly. "Have a glass of water and go back to sleep." She smiled angrily and pointed to the bathroom. Jeremy made his way to the sink and took a long sip of cold tap water, wondering if he had been asleep after all. But as soon as he looked into the mirror, he saw the same perfect circular marks lining his face and neck.

Jeremy was too afraid to talk about the thing in the basement after that night, and the rest of the family was perfectly happy not to bring it up. But still he had to know what it was, how it got there, and what could be done about it. His bed had been broken, and the vent on the wall behind it ripped off. He no longer wanted to sleep in that room or live in the Crafts' house. He would have been much happier to spend Christmas at the orphanage. The terrible smells grew fouler and more frequent each day, and Mr. and Mrs. Craft fought more and more intensely behind their closed bedroom door. Steven withdrew entirely and refused to talk to Jeremy at all. Finally, the afternoon of Christmas Eve, Mrs. Craft took Jeremy aside.

"Jeremy, you know you're a part of this family, don't you?"

He nodded nervously.

"But there is something we have to do… as a family… without you."

"What are you going to do?"

Mr. Craft and Steven sat despondently at the kitchen table staring at the basement door.

"We're going to take care of something. Then we'll sit down to a wonderful Christmas dinner. All four of us. But first I would like for you to take a long… long… walk. Can you do that for me Jeremy? Six times around the block?"

He nodded.

"Good boy."

Jeremy put on his boots, coat, and hat and took a walk around the neighborhood in the cold, gray, overcast December air. He counted six times around the block and returned to the little white house with the red brick walkway. He knocked and waited for several minutes. But no one answered. The door was unlocked, so he finally let himself in. The terrible odor was worse than ever.

"Mr. and Mrs. Craft? Steven? I'm back."

There was no answer. He checked upstairs. In both bedrooms. The bathroom. Even the closets. He called all throughout the house, but nobody responded. He wondered if they too had gone out, but the car was in the driveway. Their coats were in the front closet. Jeremy went to check the backyard and stopped dead in his tracks when he noticed that the basement door was wide open. He saw clearly down the old wooden steps for the first time to a gray concrete floor and an old green washing machine.

"Hello?" he shouted. "Is everything okay?"

He took just one step onto the staircase to get a better view. No sooner than the wood creaked did a long, inky, black tentacle whip around the corner. Within a split second, it shot up the stairs and snatched Jeremy around the waist. He shouted and struggled as it yanked him down the stairs, banging his head on the ceiling and scraping his knees against the wall. The tentacle coiled around and around him, twisting and tearing his shirt and sucking at his bare skin. He finally hit the concrete floor of the basement and at last saw it. A great big black creature growing out of the floor. Its tentacled trunk burrowing into the concrete, forming cracks and holes that led into the cold dark earth. Its long black head was pointed like a squid. Little gray tendrils wriggled beneath its mouthless noseless face. Huge dark eyes the size of car tires protruded off the sides of its head. Every which way, tentacles were shoved into the wall. The ground. The pipes. The vents. Big long muscular ones with little white suckers. Narrow gray segmented ones like enormous earthworms. Still dozens of tentacles danced freely in the air like cobras. All over its body, little white maggots burrowed in and out of its flesh. The creature tilted its head back and tendrils spread from its mouth in a starry shape to reveal a three pronged beak that snapped open wide. Rows upon rows of bloody teeth swirled down into a deep grinding abyss.

Jeremy struggled as more of the creature's tentacles whipped around his arms and legs and dragged him forward.

TWELVE O'CLOCK

Jason and Lisa were hosting a New Year's Eve party on the top floor of their downtown high rise. The young couple always threw the best parties, and almost thirty of their closest friends were crammed into the two bedroom condo laughing, singing, and drinking. The music reverberated through the walls as the guests danced wildly in the living room. It had been a long time since they had all been in one place, having this much fun, and they were savoring every second.

At nine o'clock, Jason heard a frantic tapping from the hallway, barely discernable over his state of the art speakers. He opened the door expecting to greet a guest, but instead found a wrinkled old woman wrapped in a purple shawl. She scowled and shouted flailing her bony arms in the air, but Jason couldn't hear her over the noise. He motioned for a guest to turn down the music.

The old woman spoke with a deep scratchy Romanian accent, "Why is this music so loud?! I have baby granddaughter downstairs!"

Jason recognized the woman from around the building. She had never been friendly, and some of the other neighbors suspected that she and her daughter had been stealing people's packages. Moreover, she and her family cooked strange pungent meals that often caused the entire complex to smell. "We don't mean to be rude," Jason explained, "but it *is* New Year's Eve."

"Is too loud!" the woman screeched. "You turn off this music right now!"

Lisa approached the door. "We're very sorry. We'll turn our music down. Happy New Year."

The old woman sneered at each of them, turned and stormed off down the hallway shouting and tossing her gaunt hands in the air. "If you wake baby granddaughter again, you will regret it!" They turned the music down slightly, but the party guests remained as loud as before. And soon more guests arrived with more refreshments, and the night grew even livelier.

At ten o'clock, the old woman rapped on their door again. "I ask you nice to turn off music already! Is late at night!"

"It's not even midnight yet," Jason said, exasperated. "On New Year's Eve, people have parties. You'll just have to live with it this one night."

The old woman's face turned red with rage.

"Maybe we can work this out?" Lisa offered. "Would you like to come in and have some appetizers?"

"You will stop this party now! My grandchild must sleep!"

"Call the cops you old witch!" a rowdy guest shouted.

The woman scowled, "You will wish I call cops before I am done!" She whipped around and left once more. The young couple didn't want to cause any serious problems, so they turned the volume of the music halfway down. But as the night wore on, the guests themselves became even louder and rowdier still.

At eleven o'clock, the woman banged on the door one last time. When the couple opened it, they found her smiling devilishly. "I ask you nice to be quiet. You no be quiet. I ask again, and again you wake my grandchild. You have one last chance. Turn this music off and tell these people go home, or you will be sorry."

"These are our guests, and they're staying," Jason snapped.

"We can't ask them to leave now," Lisa explained. "After midnight, things will settle down. I'm sure you understand."

The old woman snickered and held out her bony spotted hand. Her fingers trembled in front of their faces as she whispered rhythmically in a strange language.

"What is that, a curse?" Jason scoffed.

The old woman smiled. "Happy New Year!" She hobbled off down the dark hallway one last time, cackling to herself. Jason turned the music all the way back up out of spite. He encouraged their friends to scream and yell all they wanted. If their neighbor was going to be so strange and unreasonable, he had no desire to accommodate her at all. Midnight approached and the party goers stood arm in arm, singing and chanting as the clock counted down to the New Year.

"Ten!"

"Nine!"

"Eight!"

"Seven!"

"Six!"

"Five!"

"Four!"

"Three!"

"Two!"

"One!"

"Happy New Year!"

As Jason leaned in to kiss Lisa, she lurched forward and clutched his shoulders. Her body convulsed as she clenched his flesh, and she unleashed an agonized ear-splitting scream against his head. Jason's skull throbbed as Lisa slipped away from him. The oblivious crowd chattered on over glasses of champagne. Laughing, drinking, and toasting in celebration... but Jason heard nothing. Only a steady unearthly ringing.

On the floor to his right, the movements on Lisa's lips were crystal clear. Three final words to Jason, and her eyes turned back into her head for good.

ABOUT THE AUTHOR

Kevin Folliard is a Chicago area author whose works include the acclaimed videogame parody *Press Start* films and their companion web series *Press Start Adventures*. He has also published the dark fantasy novel *Jake Carter and the Nightmare Gallery*.

ABOUT THE ILLUSTRATOR

J.T. Molloy is a Chicago area artist and post production editor. Recent works include promotional materials for Dark Maze Studios in Champaign, IL as well as the action adventure graphic novel "The Sapphire Spectre."

Available by the same author . . .

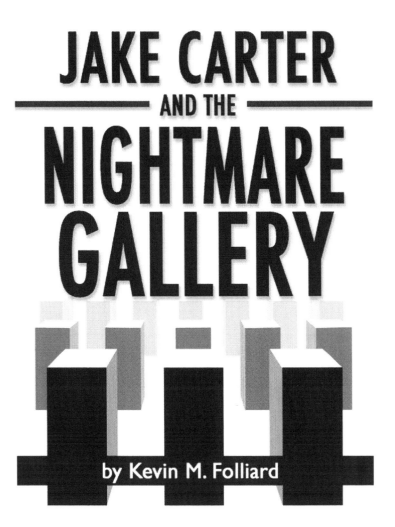

JAKE CARTER
AND THE
NIGHTMARE
GALLERY

by Kevin M. Folliard

4658301R00053

Printed in Great Britain
by Amazon.co.uk, Ltd.,
Marston Gate.